Cycles in Light

Belmont Creative Writers

Cycles in Light

Poems and Stories of Home

Cycles in Light: Poems and Stories of Home
ISBN 978 1 76109 639 6
Copyright © text individual authors 2023
Cover image: Peter Crocker

First published 2023 by
GINNINDERRA PRESS
PO Box 3461 Port Adelaide 5015
www.ginninderrapress.com.au

Contents

Introduction & Acknowledgements

The word 'home' conveys many meanings. It situates us in space and time, linking us to each other and the world. Home can speak of comfort and belonging, of struggle and displacement, of childhood hopes or adult fears.

Every month from 2017 to 2022, I met with supportive members of Hunter Writers Centre's Belmont group to workshop our individual projects and discuss writing craft. In the process, we developed a creative conversation about the unique journeys and histories that brought us together. We shared many laughs, a few tears, much learning and plenty of inspiration, for which I am grateful. Collaboratively writing our opening poem, 'Cycles in Light', was particularly challenging and satisfying.

These stories and poems are the results of exploring what home means to us, visions and experiences of places we call home: a lush garden, a father's studio, a boat in the Amazon, an Adelaide beach, a London winter, a starry sky, a mother's car, an ancestral graveyard, a hotel room or a pottery class. The pieces are as varied, colourful and complex as the authors.

We acknowledge that 'love is a verb' was first published in *Love: Lifespan* Vol. 4 (Pure Slush Books, 2021) and that 'Autumn Ghost (i)' won second prize in a Hunter Writers Centre members' competition and was first published on their website in September 2021. 'Infinite Bleak' and 'Staging Our Home' are edited from initial publication in 2017 on the ABC Open website.

Finally, we recognise the Awabakal people of Lake Macquarie (Awaba) as the original custodians of the land on which we gathered to write and edit this book, and pay our respects to their elders past, present and emerging.

It has been a privilege to lead this collaborative venture of so many talented writers. I hope you enjoy our collection.

Nicole Rain Sellers
for Belmont Creative Writers, July 2022

Cycles in Light

       My freckled skin furrows
as if life stamped a slow reveal
of biometric code, as if
a cartographer inked galactic
paths on a map this mirror loves.
       At the window, sister
gum trees holding feathered,
furred, carapaced generations
sigh with belonging. Light
       distorts through shutters,
images reverse in glass. Doors
swing open. I tread an empty
carpet-silenced corridor, leave.
       Seeking home within
my skin, I trudge into dry forest,
backpack overgrown with poems,
mind a smoky tinderbox of embers.
       My feet hurt from walking;
can we go home yet? I've tried on so many places.
Boutique life, city streets, beaches, sequins,
seams. Still nothing seems to fit – until
       I find myself in roots,
that branch I left scarred,
my name, swung in fruit
met the world upside down.
A place beyond the trees
       where palms fan the sand,
mother, father, siblings, their masses
shrinking. The clock ticks. My child
sleeps in sighs, a balmy breeze festooned
with locust hum. Life is many homes.

Curtains twist the morning.
A wooden table, a cane chair. I reach for hot tea,
take my place among cushions. My eyes
scan the garden for doves, track
        the orange sunrise disc,
cycle in light as the planet rotates,
search the mirror for meaning
until stars overcome my shadow.

Belmont Creative Writers

Flame

In our father's studio, we huddle over the light bench, make pictures with the leftovers from his stained glass windows. At gallery openings, we children run in packs, dodge through adults' legs, steal cheese and (later) wine from passing platters. We watch beauty emerge from chaos, learn the craft behind the art. Visiting someone else's studio, we watch a glass-blower gather molten sand on the end of a hollow pipe, turn toward the kiln, take a deep breath and blow. A bubble forms, is pulled from the flame, rolled across coloured rods, returned to the flame again. We children alternate between boredom and fascination. A glimpse of the finished piece with its spiralling canes, before it's rushed to the annealer. Then the process starts again. The day is long, and we grow tired. A baby begins to cry. Our harried mother bundles us into the car and we journey on, and on, the years stretching like that vase was stretched till glass and flame become a distant memory. 'Don't study art, you'll turn out just like your father.' But still, that fascination. The flame is calling.

Olivia Hamilton

Staging Our Home

I remember begging. To clean up the filth, and bag up the crap, and sort out the mess. My family is haunted by hoarding – a generation that grew up so poor they layer security in nests, sitting on treasures, settled into a brooding squat.

But only when the charity representative visited, to see if we were good people that deserved any money, would the junk get shoved into the laundry, the kitchen, the bedrooms – god forbid anything be thrown away to make space for proper places – not like a museum where things are venerated under glass. No. We didn't want to be clearly seen.

We emptied a sitting room and hallway, eyes and noses streaming from the dust, the three of us plugged up with little balls of tissue, our only defence. We scrubbed off the lingering eau-dor of fly shit, though we couldn't hide the broken pane on the living room door, or the fact that we didn't care.

When the representative came he was shown to his chair. We were hyper-alert to his face, his posture. We were horribly polite, so tense, afraid of the ghost of squalor, that he knew something was wrong. There was secret skulking around our awkward pauses and 'shut UP' glares between charming stories – booming off bare surfaces – of our bestest school friends and chummy teachers.

He knew we were hiding something but he didn't know what, and he didn't like that, or us. We made sure he would not go off course; he could not be offered tea, just a short visit to see if we were normal. Just enough time to sit tight with him, in case reality, crammed against walls and doors, threatened to hammer down, ruining our chances of a handout.

Rebecca Trowbridge

Out of My Depth

A broken line divides
the road –
       we stop to buy lipstick.

Night fills with headlights
& the musky shade of
       Pillow Talk Pink.

Dad is driving us to the
heights again, where air
is as thin as

despair – mountains – monotony.

Another party on a hill,
his preferred distance.
I can almost feel

laundry banter more
satisfying than the view.

In the doorway a man
with a red face is reciting
a poem to my stepmother.

My father is nowhere.
I look to the sky
for clarification, for a name

instead find the trough
where ice puddles
the boundaries of itself

my wrists ready to exchange
one numbing thing for another.

Ellen Shelley

Tracing Facets of Home

There was no excitement, just a dull game of Follow the Leader, bags and pillows and being bundled into the back of a car, clutching a new toy for a 'big trip'. Or to a cold railway station with blankets and yawns and hisses of steam and people's legs in the clouds on the platform. Waiting for another 'big trip' that would lead to a place to sleep. Waking in the dark, blinking, swallowing with a dry mouth, head turning in wonder, then panic: where is the leader? And then eyes adjusted to darkness and memory returned.

But not fully understanding. You were just there. It was another place.

A small gate sticks in the lock, is lifted and dragged over the path to open. The slippery, moss-covered path leads to the front door. The single key on a piece of string fits easily but the door needs to be budged with a shoulder and then a hip. Mouldy and dirty smells make us breathe through our hands held over our noses.

We all traipse through to a lounge room and stop and stare in awe at the fireplace with a wood stove, and shell-like paper windows at the front. We pass by a bedroom with beautiful metal diamond shapes in the windows. I go in and trace around the diamonds in the dust. My fingertip turns black but I love that window and the afternoon sun is making pretty, diamond colours in the glass. I don't want to leave.

The others are in the kitchen. It has a sink but no hot water and there is an old glass-doored dresser. The doors are open and there are spider webs inside, and as we open the drawers mouse droppings and more horrible smells make us shriek. We find a flower pattern on the lino floor under the dirt. There is a lot of cleaning to be done. Even the youngest agree.

The back door leads to a toilet and more spiderwebs. Then down the ramp an expanse of garden opens up to us. Gum trees stand like giants swaying limbs of silver leaves over the grassy slope below. A hill of bush beyond is filled with birdsong. We cross the garden looking up into the trees and break into a run, chasing one another in the dusky glow, excited. This will be home.

Maxine A Jacobi

Winter Morning

When winter's frosts
cold-sharpened the ground
and puddled ice
lace-edged dam and creek beds

my father was first to rise.
He lit fires in the fuel stove
and whitewashed fireplace,
our country kitchen filled with heat.

When we came in for breakfast
a saucepan of milk sat at the stove's edge.
We toasted bread on three-pronged forks
held up to the fire's glowing coals.

This was his gift;
food and warmth,
while outside
New England cold waited.

Diana Pearce

love is a verb

she loves through the door
loves into the hatchback
loves the kids to school
loves six hours at work
loving the weekly bills
loves them up from soccer
loving down the driveway
to love the preloved laundry
love a hot meal from scratch
and love four bedtime stories

they love her into the kitchen
love loudly in the bathroom
love toothpaste everywhere
love where their homework is
love their lunchboxes behind
love into fights at recess
love back home on the bus
love her like birds love sky

she loves art on the fridge
loves loose teeth and grazes
loves head lice and nightmares
loves bicycle chains back on
loves guitars loved out of tune
loves new shoes on a shoestring
loving all monsters and fairies
loves them about their opinions
loving firm when they love fires
or love rocks through windows

loves them at frisbee and cards
loves bespoke pirate costumes
loves rainbow birthday cakes
loves her shovel into the dirt
so they can love flower seeds
loves them to love themselves
to love their friends at sleepovers
love ready for their first dates
and love for their driver's licences
she loves them out into the world

Nicole Rain Sellers

Facebook Prototype 1960

My father's face was lit by the yellow glow of gauges and instrument panels. A large microphone sat on the middle of his bench in the 'radio hut' underneath the house. One wall was covered in postcards sent from Facebook friends in exotic locations, on another wall was a map of the world, and above his operating bench were photos of warships.

This space in our home was special for my brother and I. We'd run down the back wooden steps and swing under the patio into a cabin filled with electronics and intrigue. There was muted light in his shack and the smoke from his Ardarth cork-tipped cigarettes stung our eyes. It was as if we'd been transported into a ship's radio room.

He'd switched on the valves of his Ham radio fifteen minutes earlier to warm up 'the set', which was a series of home made boxes stacked one on top of the other, housing valves, condensers and coloured wires. Switches, dials and gauges were all within his reach. Muffling both sides of his head were imposing HMV ear phones.

Then he'd broadcast to the world.

CQ CQ CQ

This is VK 2AYW, testing, testing, testing.

Victor King Two Alpha Yankee Whiskey testing.

VK2 AYW, is anybody there? Over.

The CQ call was an invitation to others who were listening in that frequency to respond.

My dad explained that his voice would be transmitted up the wire above the house and out into the atmosphere through the aerial. Weeks before, he had mates from the RSL help him erect a tall, straight sapling to anchor the wire from the chimney of the house. It traversed across our backyard and was visible from the main street.

His mates from the club knew him as Jack, the ex Chief Petty Officer of Communications, fourteen years in the Royal Australian Navy. He knew about radio frequencies and band-widths from being a radio operator on ships like the HMAS *Perth, Sydney* and *Quickmatch*. Now he'd begun a hobby with amateur Ham radio, operating in short wave frequency bands.

His call sign was VK 2AYW, similar to a Facebook tag. His goal was to communicate to other radio amateurs, make con-tact, have a yarn, build up friends around the world. Just like Facebook, except the communication was aural, not written, and there were no photos shared.

We'd crowd around his desk, careful not to bump apparatus or trip on live electrical leads. My big brother Terry and I peeled our eyes on the yellow frequency dial and our ears were eager for a 'pickup' response. Dad delicately tuned the dial, and we followed the needle on the round screen until we heard a crack-ling voice from the stratosphere.

As the responder spoke in a slow American accent, my dad would fine-tune the dial to gain voice clarity, and write the call sign on his scribble pad. Then he depressed a button on the mi-crophone.

'Hello K4 APT. This is VK 2AYW calling from Bega, Australia. Jack Williams operating. Thanks for the pickup K4 APT. Do you read me K4 APT? Over.'

Terry and I watched and listened for five or ten seconds, intently awaiting a good hook-up.

'VK 2AYW. Hello Jack, this is Vince Zettervall in Duluth,

Minnesota. Pleased to have the hook-up with you, buddy. You're loud and clear, Jack. I don't get a lot of hook-ups from Down Under with our different time zones and weather. But we've got a beautiful winter night here, minus 20 degrees and clear skies. I'm operating from my shack on the edge of the woods next to Lake Superior with five feet of snow outside. Over.'

Terry and I looked at each other, eyes wide. It was hard to imagine a man speaking from America in a little log cabin amongst pine forest half-buried in snow. We were in shorts, singlets and thongs.

'K4 APT. This is VK 2AYW. Nice to hear your voice, Vince. Your signal is loud and clear. I've got two young boys listening. Sunday morning here is warm and sunny. We'll be going to the beach after breakfast. What sort of gear are you operating? Over.' The conversation continued between Dad and Vince as Terry and I tried to find Duluth on the coloured map of the world nailed with clouts to the thin masonite wall.

For every 'hook-up' Dad would place a coloured pin in a town across the globe. We had no idea where Minnesota was until Dad alerted us to the continent of North America, my first lesson in geography. Over time, I learned about countries, capital cities, rivers and mountain ranges. This, along with Dad's photo albums of naval days when he 'saw the world', ignited my passion for travel later in life.

The two men from opposite ends of the earth continued to chat about radio gear and their Ham operator histories. They compared notes about their lives, families and occupations. Names and addresses were swapped and invitations to 'come and visit any time' were extended, but visits never happened. Promises were made to 'hook up' again next month, but that didn't seem to happen either, Dad keener to find another ham operator in Scandinavia, Africa, or even a remote part of Australia. He wanted to show us how many pins he could display on his map, how many 'likes' collected on his Facebook page.

Phillip Williams

Adelaide in the Eighties

As Adelaide stretched under a stone-wash sky
the summer holidays ignited with abandon.
Teens convoyed from city to south coast
in Monaros, Beetles and Sandmans
to see bands crash and Black Russians sunk.

Spiral perms were spritzed
and lids brushed blue.
We dragged on Escort Reds
and accessorised in fluoro belts
cinching tight our bubblegum jeans.

Kombis multitasked, as bongs
and bodies bubbled inside.
Pina coladas hung in the air.
The signature of coconut
civilised in plastic cups.

Billabong branded everything.
Hot Tuna crossed our backs.
Jetties scaled our burnt feet.
Tans were mandatory on oil-soaked skin.

Towels flicked
Sarongs tucked
Noses zinced pink.
Boomer Beach rolled, sucked
and spat us out.

We *like wow wiped out* to the Hoodoos,
Slipped off our stockings and shoes to the Angels,
Shook all night long to ACCA DACCA
and while Nena played with her Luft Balloons
we were on a 'Road to Nowhere'.

Ellen Shelley

Hotel Quarantine

Radio squelch echoes up internal balconies over reception.
Outside my room, police and health workers
patrol in orange masks, duck-beak fashion.
Hey, go back in ya room! Now ya got a warnin'
and that's gonna cost ya money if ya don't stay in there!

I peer through the peephole, roused by noise
but the hall fishbowls the same carpet and doors.
Later, a paper rustle and knock pull me – Pavlov's dog –
to a conjured food bag. I call *thank you* to no one
while the larger void sweeps past my masked, barefoot pose
at the door and bag handles, inspects the room for beige
isolation then vacuums out the writer's block
as I shut on it, fond of my own quiet.

Later I hurry two blue-smocked, gloved, Perspexed Covid testers
with their hotel trolley of sanitiser, swabs, test tubes and stickers.
Ladies, I have a full day. I finally wrote three poems that
were weeks-delayed by responsibilities and distraction.
You interrupt a productive regime of meditation,
double exercise and hotel-room tea and biscuits.

I brush every tooth thoroughly; I take longer with my stretches.
I have time for body lotion. I luxuriate in the muteness
of a thirty-square-metre box. I tell friends with families
who agree this is fabulous and remember an old fantasy
shared with one, happily introverted, about booking rooms
(he with dark decor, I with high floors), no partners
nor shrilldren, TV off. Home means peace within myself
at island pace, cloistered in our own separate cities.

Rebecca Trowbridge

Up in the air

The years I travel, seeking home in other places. I arrive in Catania, that city of lava-black stone whose rhythms of life seem made for me: slow meandering walks through piazzas and cobblestone streets; people-watching from a seat at the local bar; long lunches and longer evenings stretching into night. Bright light enters through glass streaked with ash, while below, a cacophony of voices haggle over price: it is market day in the *pescheria*. Too soon, it is time to move again. In Rome, *Città Eterna*, I wander streets filled with echoes of the past, where archaeological remains can halt construction of a metro line. People talk to me of death and longing; they think the place I come from has no history. And in a way they're right: in Sydney, a light rail station is built over an archaeological site before it is even documented, burying evidence of frontier wars. History sinks into the ground, ignored, while skyscrapers reach towards the clouds. I return, feel the city trying to pull me back into its fold, but it is an uneasy homecoming. Soon, I am in the air again: Buenos Aires to Rio, Bogotá to Lima. A continent where electrical wires tangle in the air, where shanty towns multiply and bodies in bikinis dance to endless drumbeats. The relentless rhythm enters my bones. Restless, I dance on. Still not home.

Olivia Hamilton

Reconnection

Jasmine trails the fence. Tendrils grab the native ash, wrap the lavender bushes. A carpet of weeds covers pavers, creeps through crevices, hides under lush green foliage. Abundant screen bushes exceed expectations. Lavender spikes wave in a warm breeze. Native shrubs have emerged to spread and wander. Summer rains gave them their maturity. Russet branches with olive green leaves throw scents of new growth, roll in air tinged with a moist, earthy aroma. A dove lands on the garden arch. A white feather lifts on the breeze. A black-and-yellow butterfly floats among bees that bounce from lavender to blue-eyed bush blooms. No disturbing sign of my presence. I am held in a dream-like trance. Sun rays feel warm on that small area of my back that is always cold in the middle of the night. When torch lights swept and fell on walls and floors after a moan, sometimes a scream. A prison wall at night, an invisible wall of protection by day. Fight fear, build strength. The pain, the loneliness…take the medication, do the exercises…then sleep it all away. The doves coo. My home is their home. I have been too long away. My garden shows me where truth lies, peace, escape. Ground my body, keep me close and I will be sustained by home, to tend the earth, flourish and survive.

Maxine A Jacobi

Black Ice

The snow is already two inches deep and winter has barely started. Only last week, old Mrs Penny slipped on the black ice and was carted off in an ambulance. She lives in the house with the broken green lantern above the door, number twenty-one, just a little way up the street. She hasn't come home yet. Her children have been in and out a few times. I hardly recognised them. Slim young things they were the last time they walked along this street; fat and balding now. I suppose they must be near fifty themselves. Yesterday they came with a smartly dressed stranger.

Bertie Collins watched them from his window on the first floor of the house opposite. He always kept an eye on Mrs Penny; watched her comings and goings. According to Flora, in the house nearest to me, Mrs Penny played the pokies at ten o'clock sharp every day. She didn't tell me this, of course. I heard her talking to Agnes who lives next door to her. No one talks to me.

The street I live in is a short street that forks either side of my house. An old street, cobbled with no space for cars. The right fork leads down to the Singing Fox and the common; the left fork follows the arc of the old city wall and curls about the markets. In quiet moments during the day, I can hear the spruikers, and on market day, the cattle yards further on. At night, singing and fighting drift up from the tavern.

The wind whistles down the street and I curl deeper into my coat, feeling grateful for the thickness of my beard and hair, so matted that even the lice can't breathe. Snow fell most of the night, only to be trampled into slush during the busy day. It will freeze again tonight. There will be more Mrs Pennys before the week is over.

The sun always rises at the end of my street. On a clear morning, its curve slowly fills the gap previously taken by the night sky, the hill crest being unhindered by distant buildings. It shines a gleaming copper light along the cobbles and directly onto my dwelling. I sometimes think the house and street were built by a mystic or erected on the grid of some old druid temple. If the latter, I must have offended the old gods in some way.

Bertie Collins hangs his washing over the rail of his balcony. Agnes and Flora are shocked each week at the sight of Bertie's voluminous drawers spread out for all to see. The children laugh and Bertie knits his eyebrows and shows his jagged teeth in response to the prim tut-tutting coming from the ladies standing at their doorways. There was a time when the street was constantly decorated with brightly coloured laundry. It hung across the street like prayer flags on lines strung from one balcony to the other. The early evening would be filled with the squeak of rollers and gossip as clothing was slowly hauled in. That was before everyone had their own personal washing machines and dryers delivered. I think the community spirit suffered from the change. The lines had connected the families, and the fear that their lines might be cut and their washing trampled on the cobbles, ensured peace and conviviality. The street seems quite drab without the frills, petticoats and dresses blowing in the breeze.

A large van came today and began removing Mrs Penny's few bits of furniture. Bernie watched from his balcony and Flora and Agnes watched from their doorsteps. Other residents came out to stare but were quickly bored and retreated away from the cold. When the old piano came out there was a collective gasp. Bernie blew his nose with such a honk, the removalists spun their heads about mid-step. At the same time a great gust of wind blew up the street. The men staggered and the piano heaved back and forth in their grip and threatened to break free and shatter upon the stones. The piano keys clanged and thundered in a ghastly discordant tune that was offensive to the ears and surely came from the grave: Mrs Penny herself sounding a curse upon watchers and handlers alike, within a wind of ire and protest.

The ladies turned to scowl at Bernie, but he had disappeared into his room and closed the doors, red-faced and teary. A solemn occasion for us all; a final blow to the past. Every Saturday there had been parties at number twenty-one. There were five of us friends who would dance and sing about that piano. Ellen Ruskin as Mrs Penny was known then, her two brothers Eric and John, Alice the neighbour and myself. Bernie was ten years younger and excluded from our fun. Happy, hopeful days, the future, for good or bad, yet to unfold.

It is night now and the street is lit by old-fashioned street lamps on either side of where I live and where the street forks. The chimneys have been coughing great clouds of black, stinking smoke for hours. It gathers in the shop entrance where I now live and settles on my meagre possessions, filling my lungs and coating the walls of the derelict shop behind me with another layer of soot.

The living rooms along the street light up and shine over the cobbles with a promise of warmth and comfort. People go in the front door and, as if in a puppet show, appear at the window. Shadows from Agnes's house go back and forth, sometimes in a jumble or, if there are just one or two people near the window, I can make out their movements and the mood of the household.

I have a direct view into Flora's living room, although she seems unaware of this since she leaves the curtains open for much of the evening. I can just make out the dance of a lively fire. A homely sight for one as cold as I am this winter night.

As I stare into their brightly lit room I feel as though I am watching a TV serial, only slower. I see them greeting each other, petting, shouting and threatening, weeping and making up. Only the children seem to notice me and make faces through the window until Flora pulls her curtains, turning the cobbles green.

Later, the lights go out on the ground floor and then light up the room above where they keep Bernie awake with the banging of their brass bed against the wall. Flora's groans of ecstasy drift down the entire length of the street. Bernie's light goes on and Agnes can be heard thumping on their joint wall. So much objection to passion, yet there are other noises that come from that room that are of a different passion and just as loud, but no lights go on and no one bangs on walls.

Everything is quiet now. The people are abed and the tavern has closed, the drunks are no longer staggering about the streets and I am once again safe from abuse. Snow is falling heavily in large, delicate puffs. A breeze causes it to drift my way and encroach on my home within the shop entrance. I pull my thick woollen coat about me, but its dampness chills me to the bone in the onslaught of a sudden whirling wind.

Silent upon the quiet snow comes a sleek black form: Mrs

Penny's cat. She treads a high step carefully over the snow that comes halfway up her legs. She snuggles up between my curled legs and belly and I open my coat a little to accommodate her and combine our body heat. In my pocket I find my last tin of sardines and roll back the lid with its little key so we may share its contents. When we have finished, I lick my fingers and she licks her paws and we huddle together for warmth and comfort. We will survive this winter, she and I.

Jeanne Leppard

Cycling Home

Home is a backyard of space, sky, sunlight, with
grey paling fences and towering eucalypts shadowing rusty roofs.
I plant vegetables, pluck juicy nectarines and collect warm eggs,
play matchbox toys in driveway dirt with imaginary friends and
shiver from a sprinkler on fresh-cut lawn.

Home is a neighbourhood of streets, paddocks and tracks
explored on a hand-me-down bike with back-pedal brakes.
I race flotsam boats in flooded gutters,
wallow in the shallow warm river and
dream below the casuarina susurrus.

Home is a beach of warm sand, running ripples and
the exhilaration of body surfing on energetic waves.
I sun bake with zinc-creamed nose and coconut-oiled body
absorbing Buddy Holly while
lying touchingly close to a bikini-clad girl from Melbourne.

Home is unhinged as a city entices. I break comfortable bonds
with trepidation, excitement and expectation.
I flit between ateliers, share houses and flats,
suffer hangovers, pub food, blown budgets and
drift, lonely, morose and confused.

Home is an enticing woman and loving partner who
provides intimacy, companionship and clarity.
We secure jobs, an old house, a damaged Datsun and
establish a home with a backyard of space, sky, sunlight with
a blond-haired baby boy.

Home is family, neighbours and friends with
discovery through travel, books and creativity.
We nurture each other into comfortable older age and
I plant vegetables, pluck juicy nectarines and collect warm eggs
beneath towering eucalypts shadowing rusty roofs.

Phillip Williams

Flourish

Six sentinel cypress mark the edges of my small grassy patch. Their heady smell of hot pine lingers in the air and fills me with inner warmth and contentment. I give the moment my full attention and appreciation, allowing my thoughts to drift with the breeze and the clouds that scud across a deep azure sky. Light and shade come and go with the swaying treetops, and I close my eyes to watch their mesmerising rhythm through my eyelids.

I think of my childhood, so many years ago and miles away. A place imbued with a sense of ancient forests, memories of a past not lived but perceived in the air and beneath my feet; a presence still felt in quiet moments, a presence that lives on undiminished through time. The smell of coal and chimney dust, lamp light in cobbled lanes, bombed houses with memories of their own. Allotments and sparkling snails, gaslight, aspidistras and stuffed birds, a grandfather clock and old aprons. Drizzling rain and double-decker buses, tube trains and musty suits.

The call of foreign lands, beaches and sunshine, the smell of squid and chips, a harbour filled with the strains of violin and cello, narrow lanes of blue and white houses.

Deserts and overcrowded buses, chickens and shared sunflower seeds, the white eagle and the monkey, the dazzle of souks and the smell of burnt kebabs on embers.

Palms and tree ferns, warm days of sweat and happiness, breathtaking sunrises and sunsets, dramatic lightning storms, stars lost to the orange glow of lava.

Memories that clothe me, make me, harnessed by the laughter and love of friends both past and present.

Memories of my life knit about me a safe cocoon in which I flourish, not binding but supporting and secure. Balmy nights, a starry dome, the air heavy with night-scented jasmine, the click of frogs, the hoot of owls, the gentle sway of branch and frond, the embrace of love, safe, present.

Jeanne Leppard

This is my favourite place

where cormorants stand on rocks
feathers extended to dry
above a lone skua
rides air currents
on outspread wings

where the pungency
of Neptune's world
fills the salt-laden air
with odours of dying fish
and living cunjevoi

where white caps
dance on water
waving flags
of willing surrender
to a southerly's cooling breeze

where the chameleon sea
holds all the colours of the sky
and a cold winter moon
showers the ocean with icy light
feathering its sable depths

where all my presence is washed away
as rocks erode to grains I cannot count

Diana Pearce

Dark Confusion

Dreams shifted into waking thoughts. Even before I opened my eyes, I knew it was too early, still dark, the night-scented jessamine too strong. With no street lights to help, the darkness was profound and provided no shadows or lighter patches with which to distinguish the furniture or even the layout of the room.

I opened my eyes as wide as they would go but still no form emerged. There was no trace of the paintings upon the walls, the chairs or the chest of drawers, even though I knew they were there. They were always there in our bedroom.

My heart pumped a little faster with rising uncertainty. Which house were we living in? Which city? Which country? Which bedroom was I lying in? My mind flickered over all the houses I had lived in, all the bedrooms I had slept in. Which one, which one?

Impossibly, the more I stared, the darker the room grew. Not a chink in the curtaining or beneath the door to give me a clue as to its position, the shape of the room, its windows and lights, air conditioner and fan. Did it have a fan? In the absence of light all these things disappeared: a black nothing, a void with no boundaries.

My heart pumped harder still, forcing my blood about my body at a greater pace. Lie still, don't think. Perhaps you are still asleep.

I placed my hands palms down at my sides and breathed deeply to dispel my growing confusion. There, beneath my fingertips, I felt the warmth that radiated across the mattress from the man at my side. I stretched out my hand and placed it on his hot back. My anxiety subsided with a sigh of relief, and my heart skipped slightly with the joy of his reassuring presence: the man with whom I had shared all the houses and all the bedrooms, and it no longer mattered which one I was in.

Jeanne Leppard

Catalyst

I love aluminium, I use it as a metaphor
for resilience; the metal that won't rust
on contact with oxygen but constructs
a protective layer, toughened

Thank you, Ma, for embarrassments
I endured. I can brave being seen.
Thank you, in-laws, for intrusions
I refused. I learned strong boundaries.

Because bromine, a hungry element,
gnaws where it pervades.

The new neighbours want to connect
but are careless with their swearing and
That Cigarette Butt, parking in our driveway,
kinky knocking on the common wall at midnight,
toy guns for their child who wants to play fight.

Bromine and aluminium crackle and spark
aggressively polite at their screen door.
Reaction wanes to inert salt, bromine depleted
and leftover foil forms a hard little ball
and caution falls to both sides of the fence.

Rebecca Trowbridge

Movement Over Light

The old bones of this house
settled around feet, called me home.
In this far from where I grew up place

I have found an architecture
similar to my own,
the pace of humidity, steel life & stubbled paths,

a downtown cadence of misty blues
a place strong enough to hold a fall.

Disaster strengthens.
After floods, tremors & shipwrecks
a city gets up.

The resurrection of art
chilled-out on sidewalks,
cafés & abandoned space

beautifying walls into doorways
of painted light,
the murals of the sea.

Verses passed around like joints
blown into bars, our eyes stung with listening,

the crates of a past
stowed in loose arrangement
to let in the air.

Ellen Shelley

Infinite Bleak

On Wednesday, the removalists baulked off the job. The secretary called to increase the rate per hour and squawked about five hundred boxes, protective equipment and manpower. But they didn't want to do it, this company whose racket is shifting stuff.

To be fair, I'm glad I wasn't there. I'd last entered twenty years ago. They were the first to look inside the house after all that time and brought with them a clash of perception that rattled both parties.

She saw a house gutted by seven skip bins, three years of resolve, weeks of backache, forty boxes packed. She imagined her new dream house, fifteen thousand dollars already spent on architectural design; the demolition team due to start next Monday.

They saw a mountain of neglect and loneliness so confronting they'd felt their own mortality. In fact, it was really only three decades of concealing her sadness daily with ephemera; doodads that promised cheer; and though the floor was completely buried, the edges of her drab despair always showed a little, here and there.

The great grey elephantine funk in the room, chaotically festooned, now overdressed, tried to shrink from the commotion. But she saw it all: her glumazon still needed to diet.

She thought the removalists were insulting; they thought she was crazy. She closed the door after their shocked backs and then called me to cry. And I heard for the first time in ages the return of the Other Self, that faint voice, deeply exhausted, who could stay in bed for days: 'Thank you, dear, I don't need your help, I'll do it my way.'

In her voice, I heard my cue to give up, to let her rest. To perhaps accept, despite decades of struggle, the old nightmare of her corpse in that grunge and the inherited clean-up. But we shared a laugh before she hung up: she'd freaked out two grown men with just a glimpse of Infinite Bleak. Honestly – hadn't they seen hoarding before? I was amazed at their naivety and then our own scoffing response.

Now I wonder, was this just the farce to launch a thousand skips?

Rebecca Trowbridge

Repatriation

I sought a place of escape
far from my city life,
my past discarded like clothes
to the Salvation Army,
took refuge in a new house,
secure in a gated community
with set colours,
prescribed plantings,
verdant lawns and a swimming pool;
a monochromatic enclave
where the ageing discuss
facelifts and Viagra® over morning tea.

Today I sit in a street-side city caf´
at one of its motley tables,
order a cappuccino and blueberry muffin.
There is a faint smell
of car exhausts, coffee and bacon.
I watch the passing atlas of faces,
listen to a towering babble of dialects
taste the richness of the blend.

Diana Pearce

Moon Bathing

In the darkness, my eyes are drawn to the most dazzling jewel. I want to believe it's you whom I miss most. In growing enchantment, feeling protected, I search the Milky Way for familiar star marks.

The moon casts a glow over the garden and my skin is tinged with gold. I wipe the backs of my hands but it stays, makes me want more of the soft film covering my skin. I peel off my jacket, exposing arms and neck. I recline on one chair and raise bare legs onto another.

Moonbeams bathe my body as I stare into my home sky. I'm drawn from above, lifted, weightless in the starry night. Are you there looking down at me?

The child has crept out again and paces the vast garden. Questions pour out with her tears, and she calls, 'Help me! Sorry, I'm not strong enough. What will I do? I wish you were here. Why does it have to be so hard?'

And it begins all over again. She looks to the brightest star. It sparkles like a precious jewel, and she is transfixed by its unique glow. Slowly the tears will subside; she'll know what to do and she will be strong.

A breeze stirs. The dry leaves of creaking tree branches scratch the paved ground. Vague floral scents linger in the night air. The light has dimmed and my gold tinge vanished. I shift in the chair. A white cloud nestles in my patch of sky, resembling an ancient skeleton swirling over my nocturnal home. I feel a timeless comfort, a soft, internal glow, a connection between earth and sky where I dwell.

And I have found my strength in peace.

Maxine A Jacobi

Wet season in the Amazon

We travelled together, back when this thing called 'we' began. You from your northern island, with its endless forms of rain. Me from my harbour city, where wavelets glisten in the sun. Boats carried us along the river that stretched like a spine through the forest. There, water was a rising thing, swallowing trees and towns. The currents carried secrets to the shore. Swinging in hammocks, surrounded by other swaying bodies, on the boat I found not peace, but a claustrophobic's nightmare. We paused for a time in a riverside town. A gust of swirling wind stole our roof, sent water gushing onto our bed. We travelled onwards, breathed in the river and the rain. The river's deceptive smoothness showed the world its inverse image. Its endless flowing presence invited confessions. *I am unsure,* I whispered. *I don't know how to be a 'we'.* The river remained silent. But when we reached the end, ocean waves, grey and heavy as the storm-clouds above, murmured like waves back home. I listened to the ocean's voice, found comfort in its inevitability. No one can stop the tide. I wonder, did you find that same comfort in the rain?

Olivia Hamilton

Autumn Ghost

After Olive Cotton, *Skeleton Leaf* (silver gelatin photograph, 1964)

i

You wink and dissolve in sepia
mulch underfoot, a velvet
of bark and twigs, ash and fog.
Spring will weave something dewy
from the vacated spiderweb life
you cast across my path, will wrap
this house in ivy, glisten snail trails,
swell snow peas, drip into my coffee,

push me to the beach to find in sand
your skeleton, some permanent imprint
of whole leaf, snowflake or spiderweb.
You planted heirloom seeds, grafted
your gametes on my spine, your shape
refracted and scattered in droplets
wherever I swim, patterned in liquid nets
or frozen steam, according to season.

My moth-eaten, backward heart dives
for the rules you made, unearths a family
tree mirrored in seaweed and leaf litter,
blood and bone, roots wider than its branches.

ii

I trace wedding lace on engraved silver
photographs, sip from your chipped cup,
scan an iron sky while wearing your beanie.
Capillaries script my lungs, pulse, summon

cold air. Inspiration straight from your mouth
will not expire but echo in other cries, whorl
in future fingerprints, flash inside storm clouds,
move under amniotic surf. Vestigial lizard tails
will sprout in summer, offshoot generations
will branch and fork, streams cross, leak brine
in freshwater brooks, join brackish rivers, fill seas
with grand plans. Your salted window tints my view;

outside, crows sketch faint guidelines. I squint at the way
you shield us, divide us, define us, your fragile, unbreakable
blueprint revealed in dirt and time, cartilage never barer
or more lucid than in winter. I want to wade in your glass
and fade like a white owl's wingbeat, but I stay distinct,
a cellulose lattice, my ridged veins black, a snowflake
poised over the ocean, a porous leaf not yet released.

Nicole Rain Sellers

Homeland

My Sister, you dwell under another sky
You lie on different earth
You tend trees with rich scents, wild fruit
broad leaves that brush the heat of day

You cool

Thick grasses decorate your path
grey-green ribbons lashing legs
Tangled bushes spring against arms
Fiery flowers flash on vines

You pass

Dust settles on your face
as hands grasp roots locked in soil
Seeds and nuts wait for you
in secret seasonal storage

You breathe

swamp-heavy air, fleshy and lush
Bright reeds, wild floral faces
You gather finest growth,
gardening to regenerate

You taste

cool water fresh from a spring
mixed with the salt on your skin
From squeezed pulp, rich colours
run sweet juice on homeward hands and feet

My Sister, you prepare and serve
a feast to share
You give thanks
I give thanks
for our land

Maxine A Jacobi

The Garden

I stood at the edge of the pavement and gazed at the row of terraced shops with a sense of déjà vu. Each shop had a large window at street level. The flats above had two windows that overlooked the busy high street. It occurred to me that they looked like a row of mouths and eyes, except the last one, which was boarded up, sightless and silent. Beside it was an empty block where an 'unlucky' house had been taken out by a German bomb, leaving its companion unstable and forever empty.

Being a sunny morning with little else to do, I decided to explore the vacant lot and see what lay behind the silenced house next door. I scrambled over grass-covered rubble left by the house's hasty removal, toward a stuccoed wall visible from the street. It formed a square that jutted out from the house, a typical backyard for this area. A small pillar of bricks rested conveniently against the wall and I stood on it to see over. Instead of the usual shed and concrete was a mass of greenery. Weeds grew wild, which at first seemed no different to the neglected vacant block.

I heaved myself over the wall and landed amidst tall weeds with small, fluffy seed heads at their tips, instantly in a place of magic. The droning traffic was now scarcely audible, and even the passing rumble of a train seemed to skim over the walls. Squatting between the prickly stalks, I listened to the near silence and enjoyed the sense of peace that filled this small space. Strangely, I wanted to stay here forever, yet at the same time to run away.

To my left, the back door stood ajar, victim to invasion by curious children or homeless adults, its small panes of coloured glass broken. Some had fallen whole to smash upon the concrete strip below; others were blown or bashed out, leaving jagged, dangerous edges. I stood slowly and stomped onto the back porch where windows either side had been boarded up, several thin planks of wood fallen, some hanging useless on a nail.

Below the windows, pots formed a scalloped trim along the brick line, many shattered into terracotta shards. Grass bulged from soil that had burst through concrete fissures. Along the row, one crack bulged not with grass roots, but bulbs. Several had shoots but the biggest stood upright, its white bell lighting up the garden and my heart.

I looked for more real flowers. The yard seemed a tangle of straggly plants, but closer inspection hinted at what had once been a garden tended with care and love. Red and yellow wallflowers and geraniums peeped out through the long grass, dock and nettles. My eyes followed the clumps of colour. Against one wall, and nearly smothered by a rambling rose covered in small blood-red flowers, was the biggest lavender I had ever seen, almost a tree. Wild lupins of mauve, pink and yellow waved in harmony with the nettles on a gentle breeze. Pink foxgloves and hollyhocks stood tall above the grass and white daisies with purple centres leant out into open patches.

I turned and poked my head inside the doorway to sniff the air. The smell of urine, old clothes and burnt wood puffed back at me. All signs of use; somewhere to sleep or a children's playground. Derelict houses were always fun to pass the time in, with familiar things like stairs and cupboards, tables or chairs left in ruins and strangely fascinating. And no one cared if you scratched the wall, or stamped in one of the wooden steps, or banged a cupboard door. A sense of freedom and daring lived in these places, and often warmth, if you stood still long enough to feel it. Layer upon layer of previous occupants and families lingered in the air, embedded in the walls, vibrating softly in floorboards that had borne the endless passing pressure of little and big feet.

A fleeting familiarity overcame me. I thought I saw the house anew: clean and fresh, with furniture, the smell of polish, shiny brass rods upon the carpeted stairs, the sound of laughter.

I stepped out into the grass, careful to avoid the nettles, and tripped on a brick border. Studying the ground more closely I was able to pick out the faint impression of a path. It ran in a horseshoe around a central bed of jasmine and dahlias that struggled to be seen amongst morning glory and yellow-flowered pilewort. The bed rose slightly in the middle, and on inspection I found the remnants of a great vase or bird bath. All that remained was the base, the bowl stolen or in pieces somewhere. Searching for signs of it, I noticed an old log in one corner. Moss glowed on its side and drew me like a moth to light. The top surface was smooth with use and quite clear of debris, so I sat without fear of ruining my clothes.

From here the garden appeared layered. A gentle mist hovered over the soil and around the base of plants, its luminosity reflected in the layers above, leaves and stems sparkling with drops of moisture. Sunlight bathed the blooms, made seed heads shiver and whisper secrets I could not hear.

I began to feel tired; more tired than I had ever been. It came on quite unexpectedly and I wondered if I was ill. I looked down at my hands, youthful just moments before, or so I thought, and found them bent and blotched with age. The ground-hugging mist shifted and called in its silent way, preventing me from dwelling on this disturbing metamorphosis. It was then that the dandelions came into view. Like my aged hands, they had not been there a moment ago. A bed of beautiful yellow faces; a thousand suns reaching up into the blue sky. Dotted amongst them, seeded heads swayed and bobbed, occasionally releasing their charges into the air like a burst of fairies into the light.

Their sun-like features reached for me and I left my log, bent and aged now, to lie down on their bed of glory. The ground mist washed over me, a blanket of peace, and bees droned a protective cover above me. With a sigh of utter contentment, I released myself to the small pads of yellow petals.

Jeanne Leppard

Nine Mile Beach With Disintegrating Woman

i

I avoid golf course crows
sleek prospectors   bloated on coal and steel
Pilots spot Sunday parachutes
my shadow   a tiny footprint beeline
but can't feel the slag grate my heels
can't hear   Moon Island cut through spume
teeth snapping at surf ski blowflies
Above   golfers circle flags   sink balls
Below   beach digests bubbles   a brain absorbing words
A sea goddess   hisses *You are a part*
clutches   releases *No more   no less*
swells   mixes   splits apart   *A part*
More   or less   all   the same

ii

Storms crack in Redhead's rock beak
Whose wings fold trees? Whose tail fills creeks?
A sea goddess   disembowels the slope
I shore myself up   woman versus water
taste mineral spray   wade in to watch
her dark lips curl   her silver hair thrash
her long arms scoop   boom upward plumes
I run for dunes   Whose pine posts dangle
foundationless? Whose wire entrails spill?
Below   her innards churn   foam bile
spat jet gallstones   kelp bladderwrack
cunjevoi sea squirts   Whose purple sacs trail
hairy-lipped mussels? Whose lung sponges blush?
Note to self   *Bring a plastic bag for plastic*
bait wrappers   cigarette lighters   fishing lures
Breathe negative ions   Purge microbeads
Whose tar veins crumble   in the bitten cliff?
Clots drop from clay   sedimentary fists   hearts
spleens   kidneys   knotted with spinifex nerves
Who reclaims the green? Disgorges rubble? Eats tarps?
Golfers squint down but can't see   coal glitter the sea floor black
can't smell her bitter rips recoil   can't hear her breath
shred the clouds   Moon Island spotlit in sun

Nicole Rain Sellers

Belonging

Outside a grey village
where cows now graze
an ancient graveyard,
lichen-covered headstones awry.

There I read
my ancestors' names
blurred on hard grey markers.

No Damascus revelation
of light and understanding,
only a subtle belonging.

Diana Pearce

From the earth

I visit that place where I took my first steps. The river flat with its cool, damp sandstone, brackish water pooling with the ebb-tide. Mangroves claim the mud, while she-oaks climb tall on the bank above. I pause, eyes caught on a vein of reddish clay. I turn away; ignore the earth's call. Years pass. Another journey; another river. The clay, here, is a deep, muddy brown. We take a tour: the leatherworks, where a busload of tourists interrupt our pretence that we are somehow different; a pottery, where the potter invites me to sit at his old kick wheel. Why does this scare me so? My fingers reach, take a pinch of clay, begin to form an off-centred bowl. My hands – my hands remember how this feels. I smile wide, pose for the camera. Feel a shadow-self grinning from the past. The return home is easy; the next step is not. I enrol in a class, but almost don't go, echoes of old scars loud in my head. 'What's the point of making art?' It will take years, yet, to silence their cries. But this first victory is the sweetest. I enter the classroom. Take a seat at the wheel. Almost get up and walk out again. No; stay; rest your busy mind and just breathe. No more running. Hands deep in clay, I can finally say, I am here.

Olivia Hamilton

About the Authors

Originally from Sydney/Eora, **Olivia Hamilton** has lived in Catania and Rome, Italy, and now makes her home in Port Stephens/Worimi country. She writes poetry, fiction and academic essays that explore the experiences of chronic pain, mental illness, and neurodivergence, as well as the political and social aspects of issues like climate change, identity and human/non-human interactions. Her poem 'time lapse' appeared in Red Room Poetry's 2022 anthology *Admissions: Voices within mental health*.

Maz Hind, raised in a loving family, has set up residence many times in three different cities, and realises that home is what lives in one's heart and not where one lives. After a career in IT and travelling extensively, she now enjoys exploring her literary, creative side, and writes short stories and poetry when inspired.

Maxine Jacobi has loved writing fiction since childhood, when she lived a jolted family life around city, country and coast. She has made Awabakal land in Lake Macquarie her home. She wrote for ABC Open, recorded stories for ABC radio, read at Newcastle Writers Festival and was twice a finalist in Hunter writing competitions. On joining Belmont Creative Writers, she became inspired by the poetic form, and now writes both prose and poetry.

Jeanne Leppard grew up in London, UK. Drawn by a tremendous desire to see the world and make it her home, she donned her pack and set off overland by public transport as far as Calcutta. That particular journey ended in Sydney. Australia is currently her home, but the wider world still beckons. She is published in *The Story Hunters Anthology*, Volume 2 (Hunter Writers Centre, 2021).

After retirement from a successful career in education, **Diana Pearce** renewed her love of creative writing, especially poetry. At the University of Technology Sydney, she completed her Master of Arts in Professional Writing, which included a collection of poems. Diana continues to participate in courses and attend workshops. Her poems have been published in magazines and anthologies and awarded in competitions. In this collection, her thoughts of home flow from farm to beach to graveyard.

Nicole Rain Sellers was born on Lenni Lenape land near Philadelphia, USA, grew up on Dharawal land near Sydney, and has made her home on Awabakal land near Newcastle, Australia. She co-authored *Fossilised Lightning* (Girls on Key Press, 2021) with Rebecca Trowbridge. Her writing has been awarded or listed in Australian prizes and appears in anthologies and journals. She is currently researching contemporary eco-spiritual poetry at the University of Newcastle. www.nicolerainsellers.com

Ellen Shelley, raised in a family of step-siblings with a procession of stepmothers, soon learnt the art of resilience and the importance of finding a home for herself in the world. She has been published in *The Canberra Times* 2018 and 2019, Highly Commended for the Philip Bacon Ekphrastic 2019, *Cordite* 2019, Manly Spirit of Renewal 2021, Queensland Flying Arts Ekphrastic 2021, *Women of Words* 2022, *Rabbit Poetry Journal* 2022, and various anthologies.

Rebecca Trowbridge juggles law study, family and writing. She has spent time as an army corporal, geologist, market research caller, ski lodge manager, university tutor and high school teacher, while living and working around Australia from the outback to the coast. Her poetry collections include *Escaping the Timeline*, *Fossilised Lightning* (co-authored with Nicole Rain Sellers) and *Bitter Matriarch*. www.rebeccatrowbridge.com

Phil Williams came to fiction, memoir and poetry late in life, believing that creativity through written expression was a purposeful activity for retirement. Much of his yet unpublished writing is based on his wide experience of work, travel and family life. His childhood home, school and neighbourhood are rich sources from which he draws.